Boffin Boy and the Quest for Wisdom

By David Orme
Illustrated by Peter Richardson

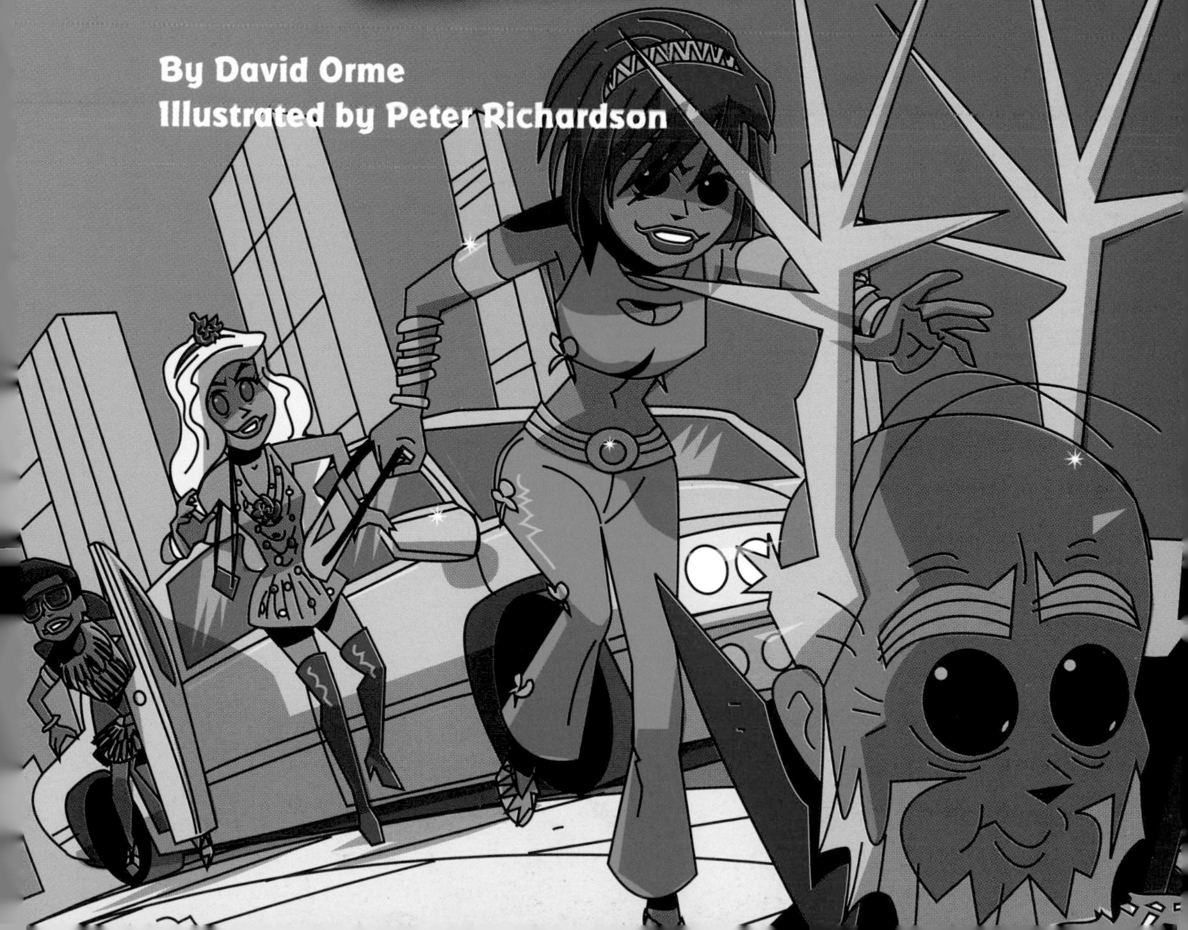

COLLECT THE SET!

Boffin Boy and the Invaders from Space
978 184167 613 5

Boffin Boy and the Wizard of Edo
978 184167 614 2

Boffin Boy and the Monsters from the Deep
978 184167 615 9

Boffin Boy and the Red Wolf
978 184167 616 6

Boffin Boy and the Lost City
978 184167 617 3

Boffin Boy and the Time Warriors
978 184167 622 7

Boffin Boy and the Ice Caves of Pluto
978 184167 626 5

Boffin Boy and the Quest for Wisdom
978 184167 628 9

Boffin Boy and the Deadly Swarm
978 184167 625 8

Boffin Boy and the Rock Men
978 184167 624 1

Boffin Boy and the Temples of Mars
978 184167 623 4

Boffin Boy and the Forest of the Ninja
978 184167 627 2

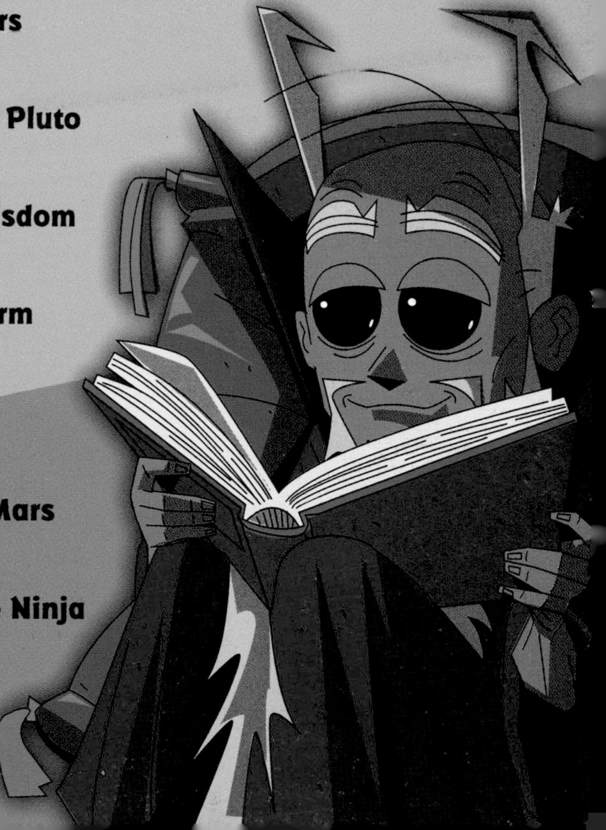

Boffin Boy and the Quest for Wisdom
by David Orme

Illustrated by Peter Richardson

Published by Ransom Publishing Ltd.
51 Southgate Street, Winchester, Hants. SO23 9EH
www.ransom.co.uk

ISBN   978 184167 628 9
First published in 2007
Copyright © 2007 Ransom Publishing Ltd.

Illustrations copyright © 2007 Peter Richardson

A CIP catalogue record of this book is available from the British
Library.

The rights of David Orme to be identified as the author and of
Peter Richardson to be identified as the illustrator of this Work
have been asserted by them in accordance with sections 77 and
78 of the Copyright, Design and Patents Act 1988.

Design & layout: *www.macwiz.co.uk*

Find out more about Boffin Boy at *www.ransom.co.uk.*

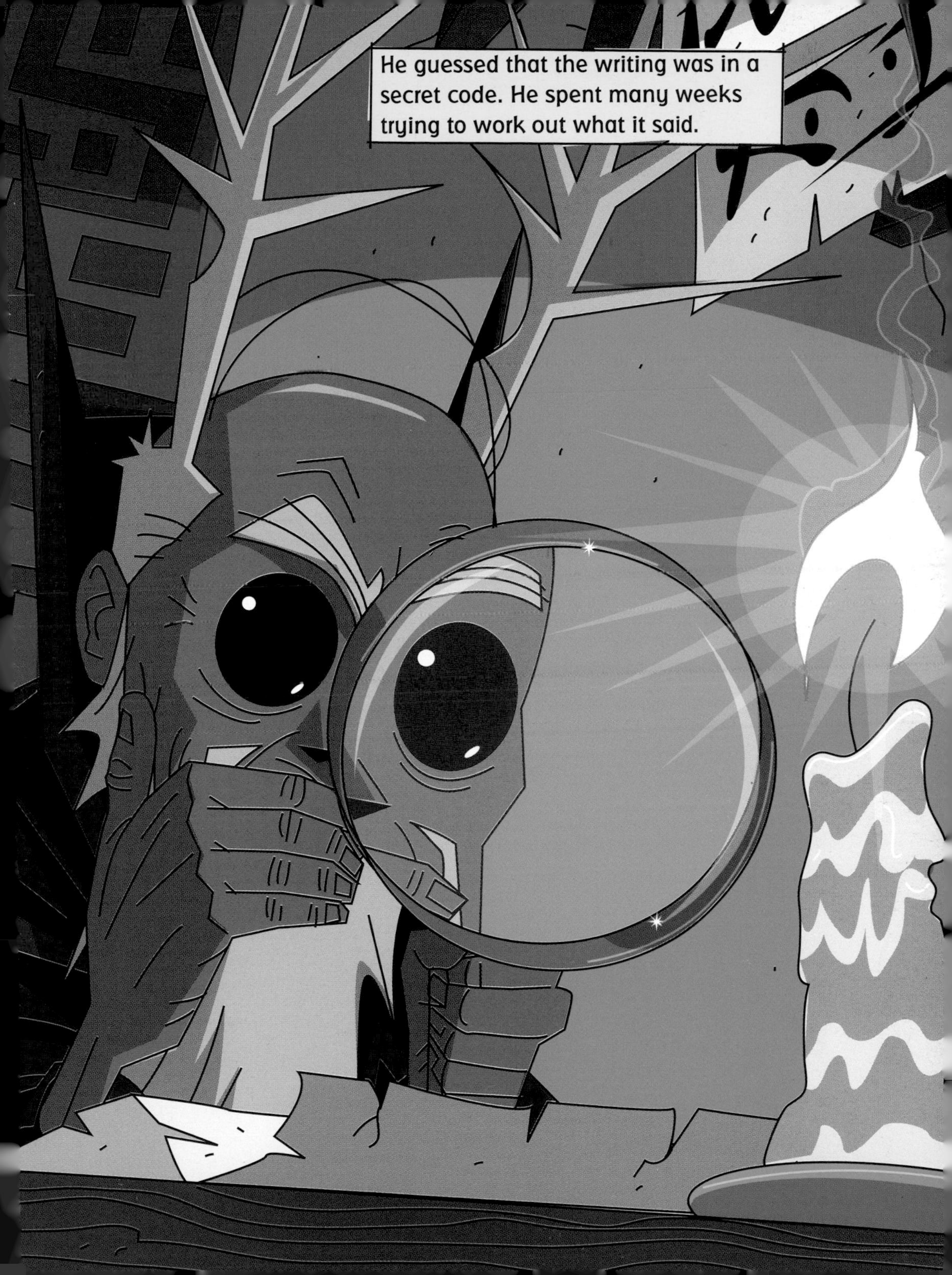
He guessed that the writing was in a secret code. He spent many weeks trying to work out what it said.

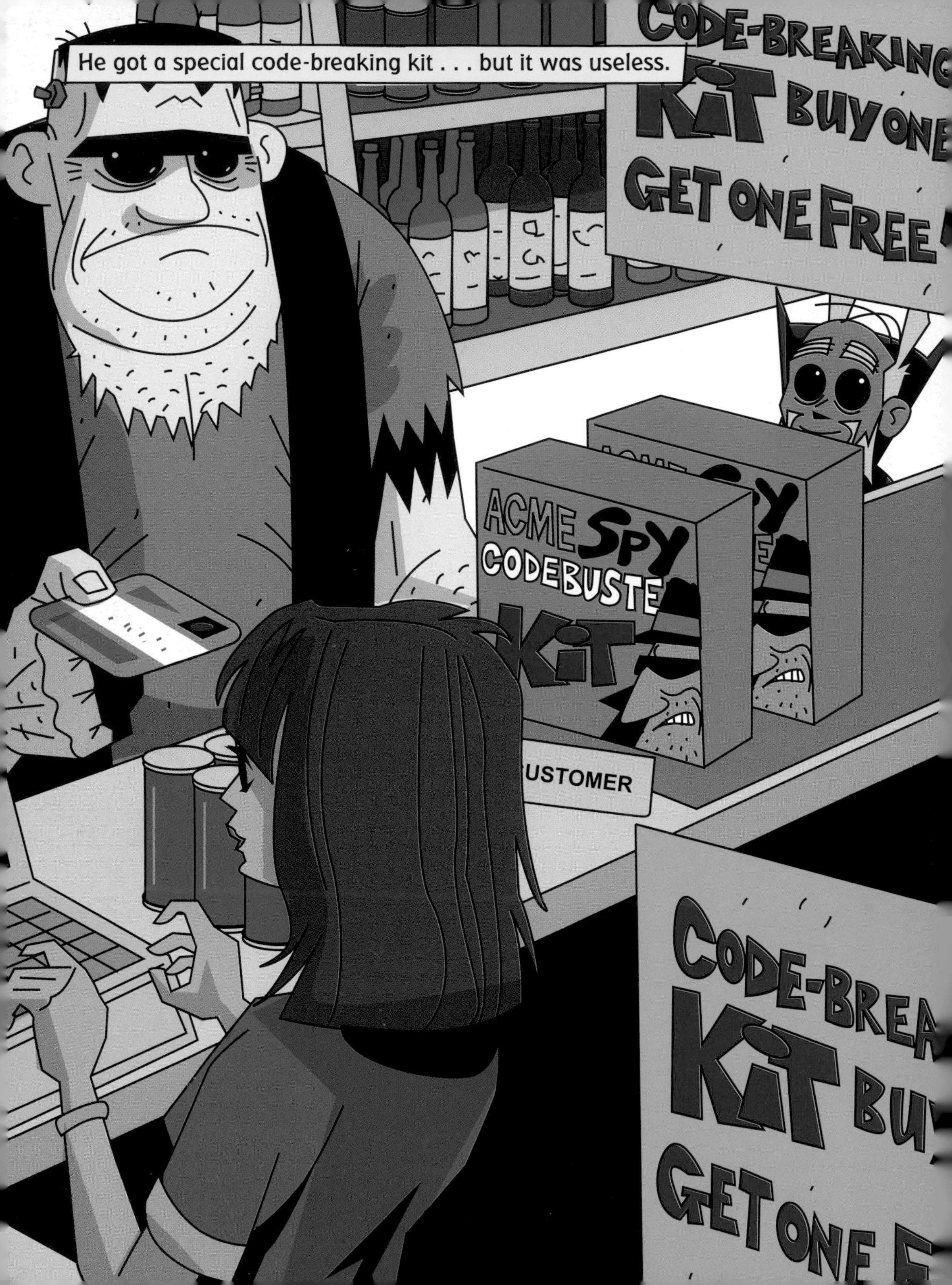

He got a special code-breaking kit . . . but it was useless.
CODE-BREAKING KIT BUY ONE GET ONE FREE!
ACME SPY CODEBUSTE KIT
USTOMER
CODE-BREA KIT BU GET ONE

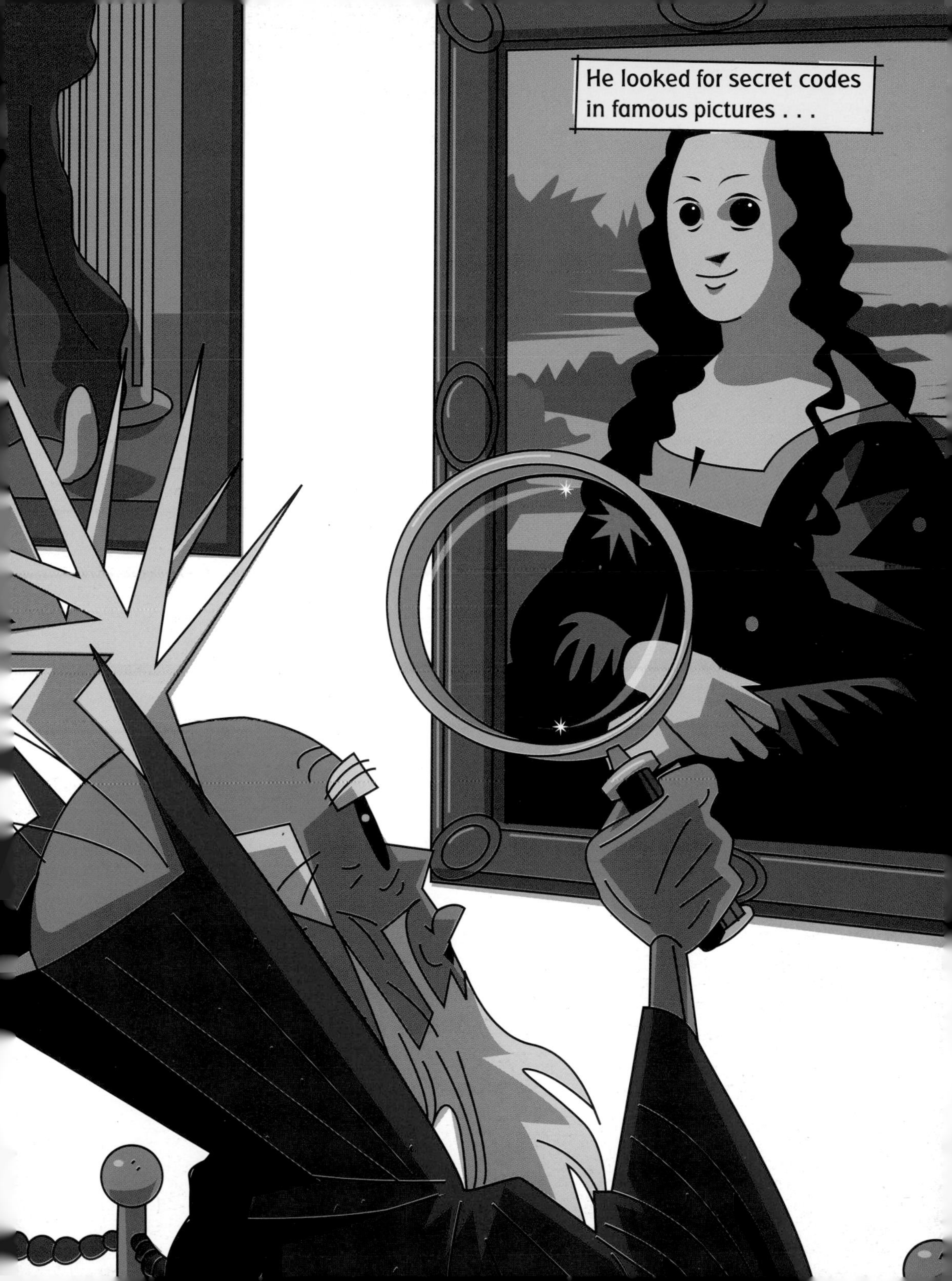
He looked for secret codes in famous pictures . . .

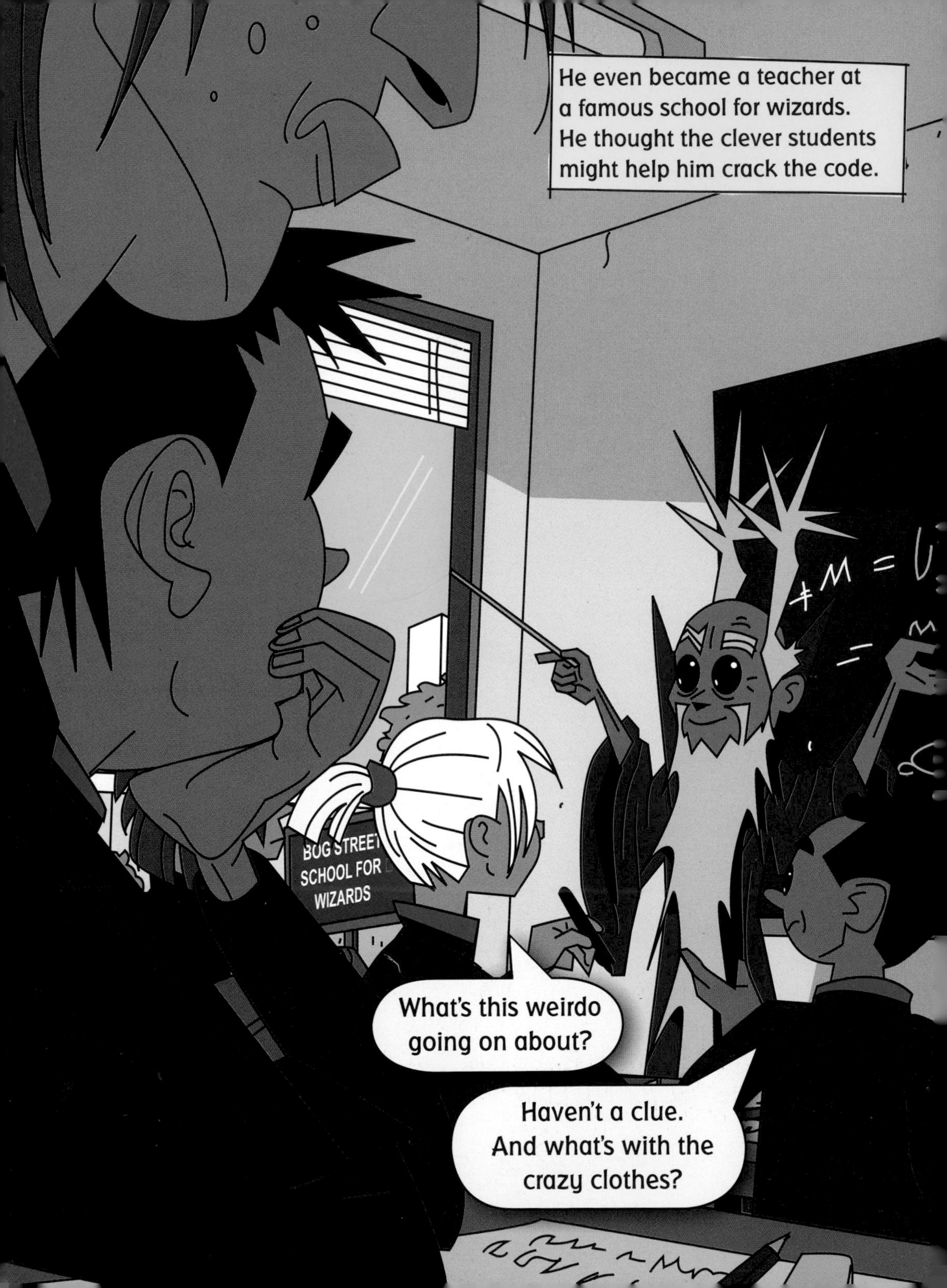
He even became a teacher at a famous school for wizards. He thought the clever students might help him crack the code.
BOG STREET SCHOOL FOR WIZARDS
What's this weirdo going on about?
Haven't a clue. And what's with the crazy clothes?

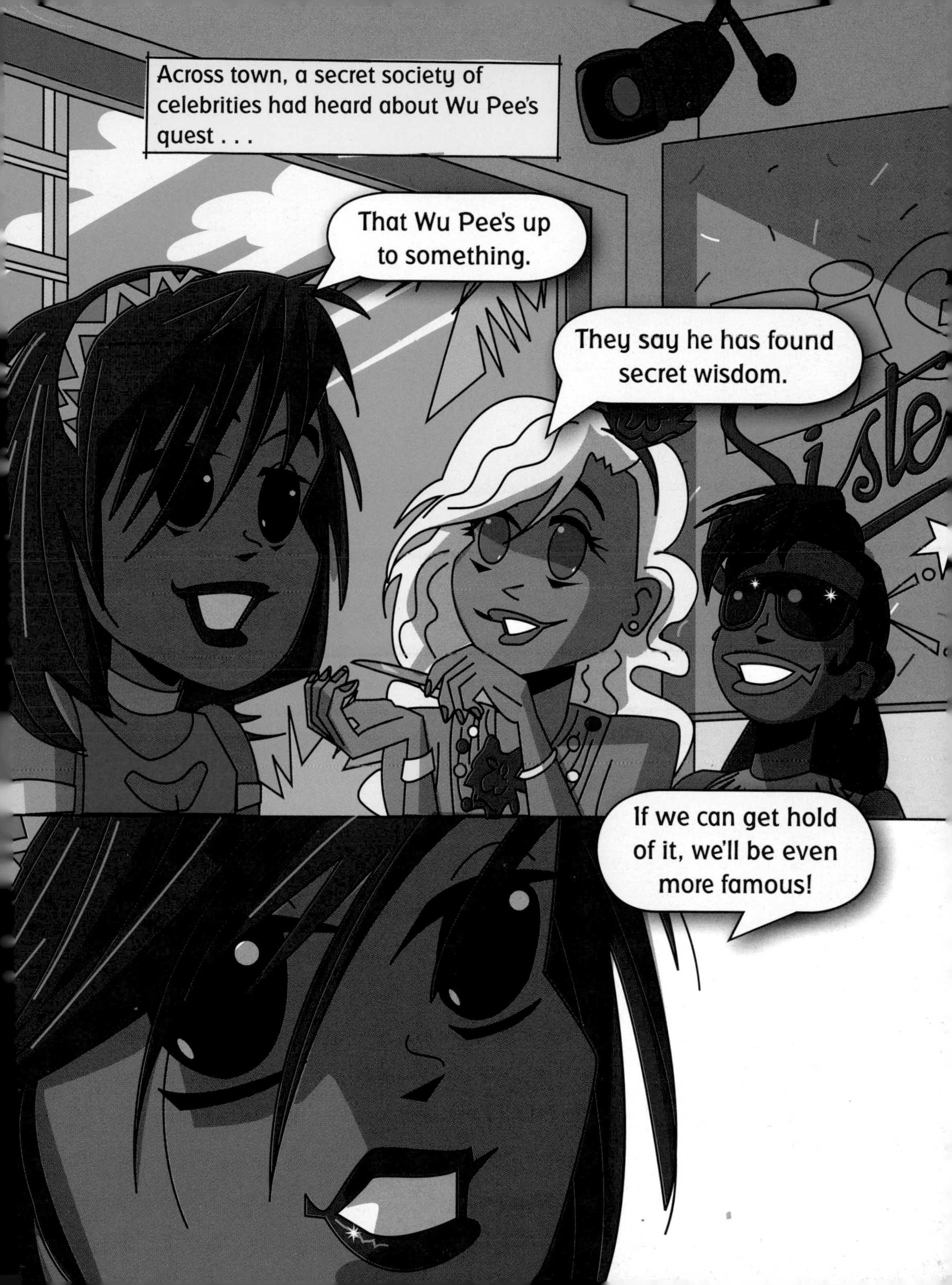
Across town, a secret society of celebrities had heard about Wu Pee's quest . . .
That Wu Pee's up to something.
They say he has found secret wisdom.
If we can get hold of it, we'll be even more famous!

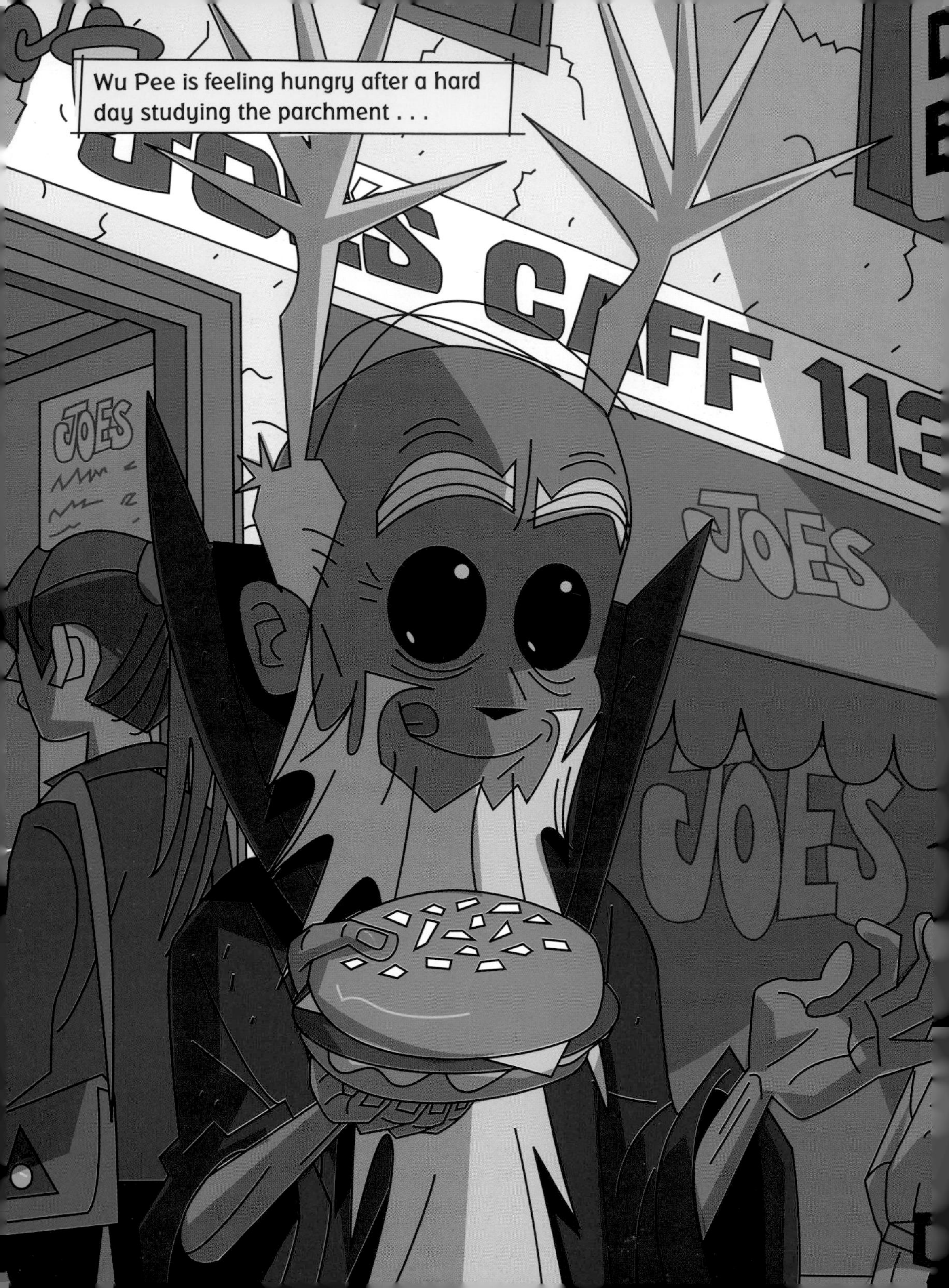
Wu Pee is feeling hungry after a hard day studying the parchment . . .
CAFF 113
JOES
JOES
JOES
JOES

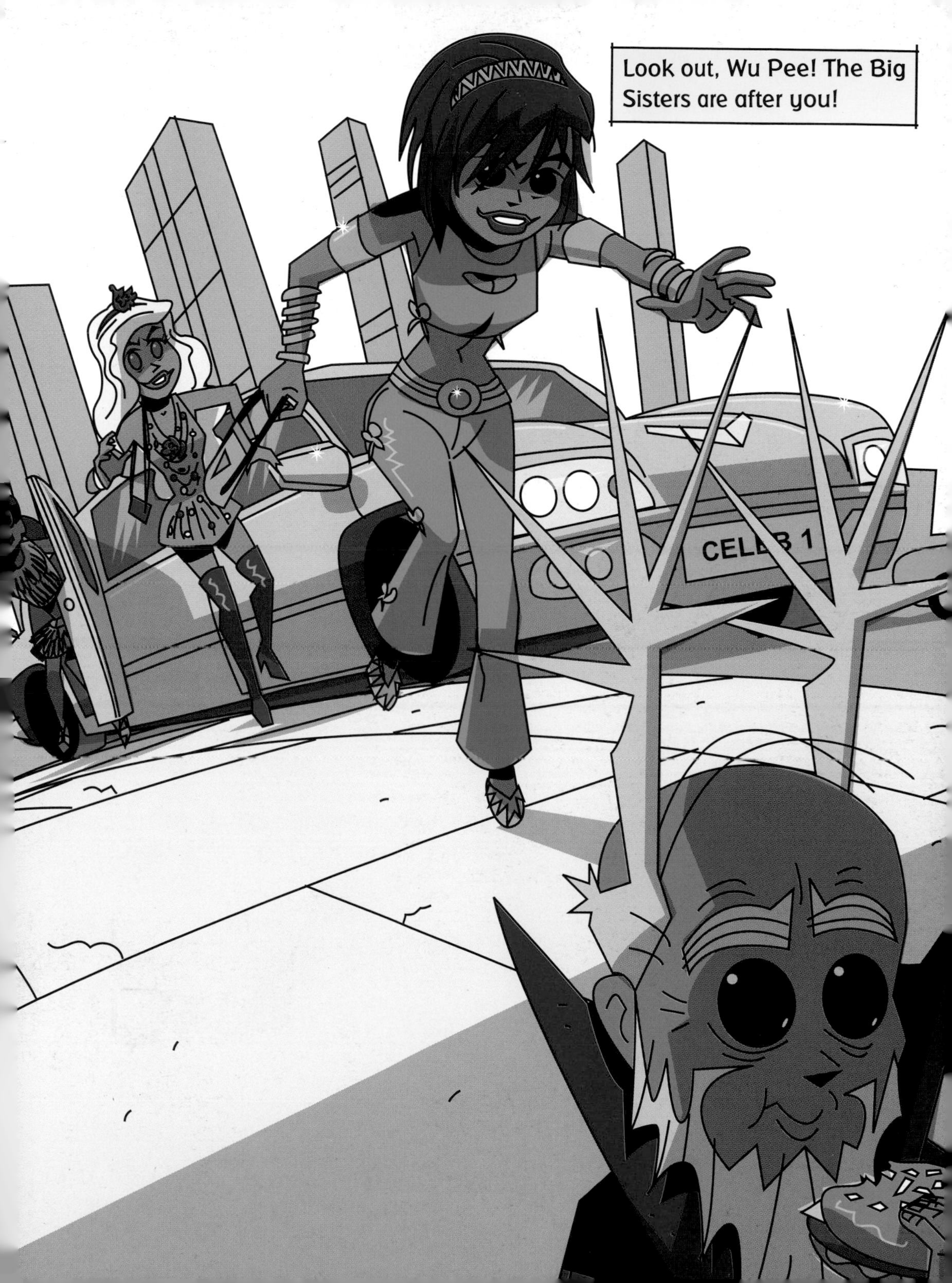
Look out, Wu Pee! The Big Sisters are after you!
CELEB 1

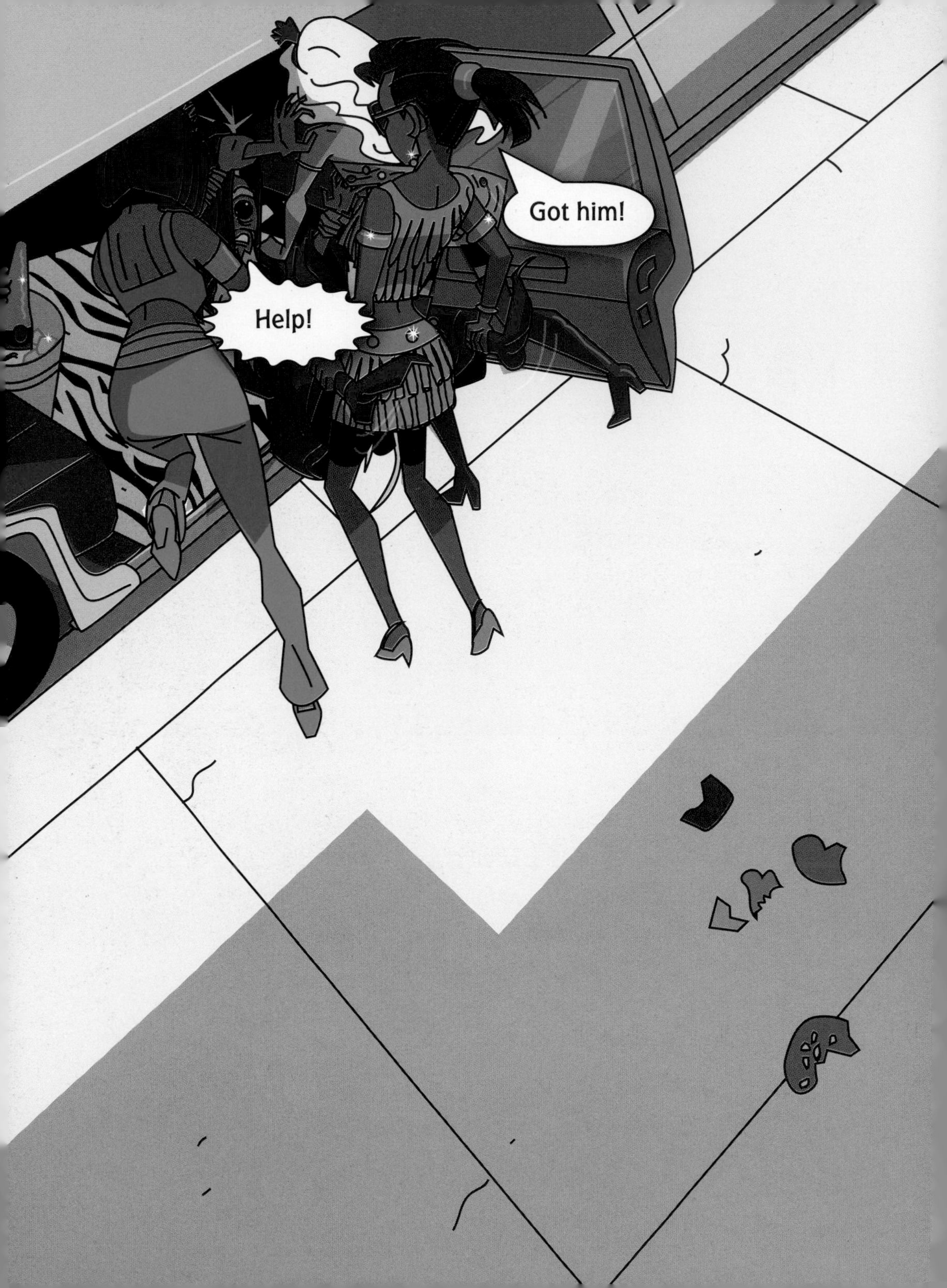
Got him!
Help!

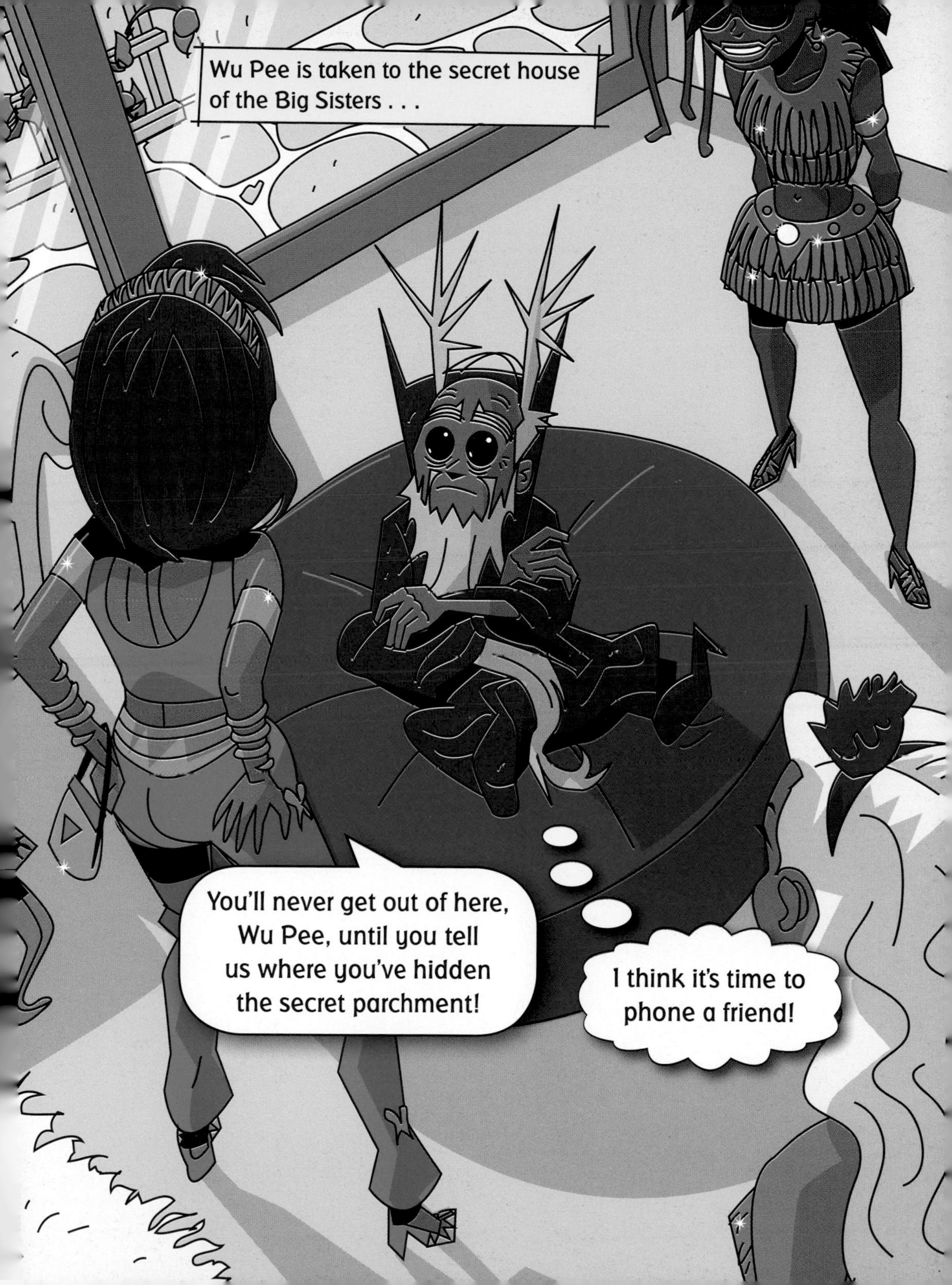
Wu Pee is taken to the secret house of the Big Sisters . . .
You'll never get out of here, Wu Pee, until you tell us where you've hidden the secret parchment!
I think it's time to phone a friend!

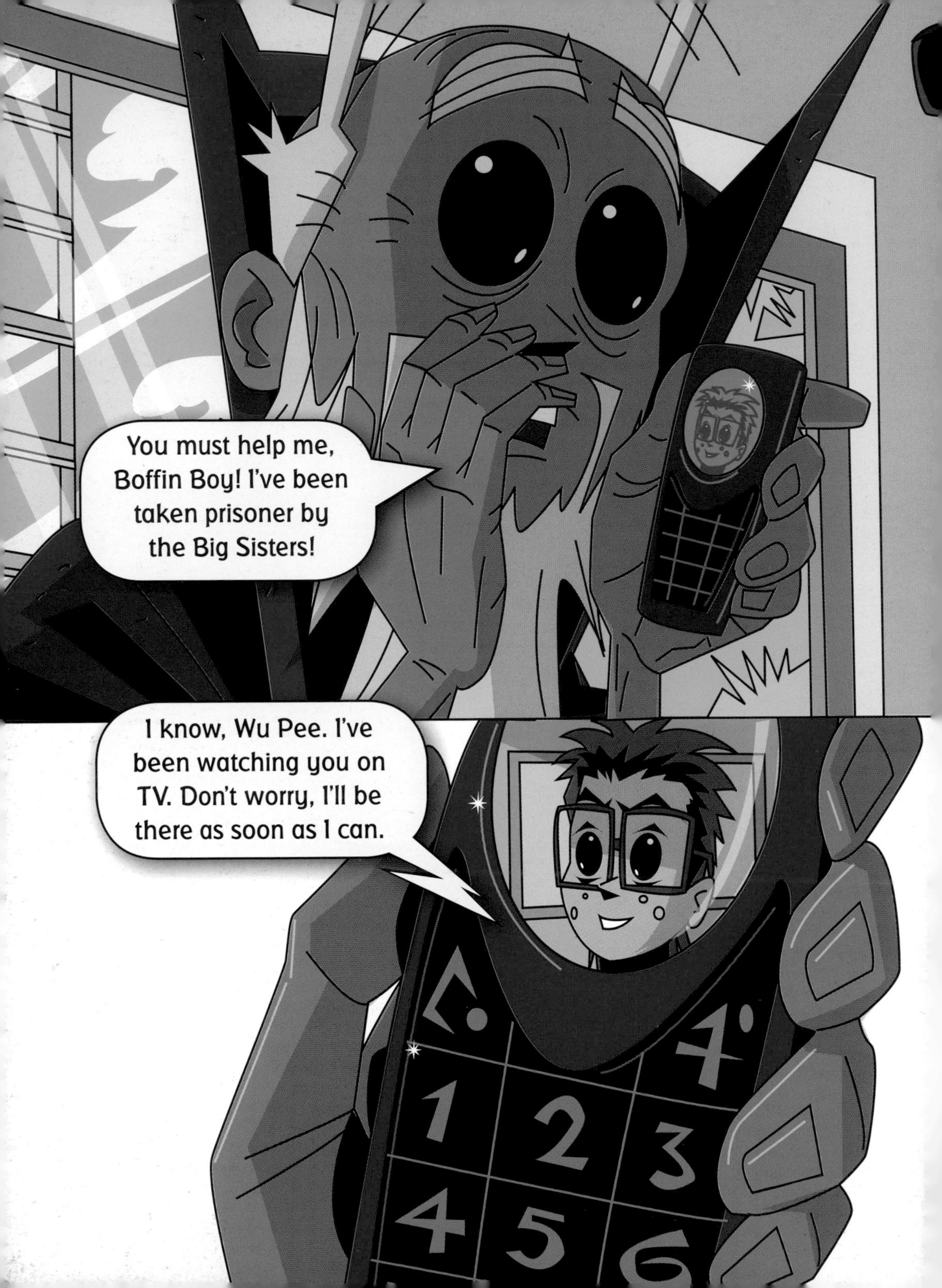
You must help me, Boffin Boy! I've been taken prisoner by the Big Sisters!
I know, Wu Pee. I've been watching you on TV. Don't worry, I'll be there as soon as I can.

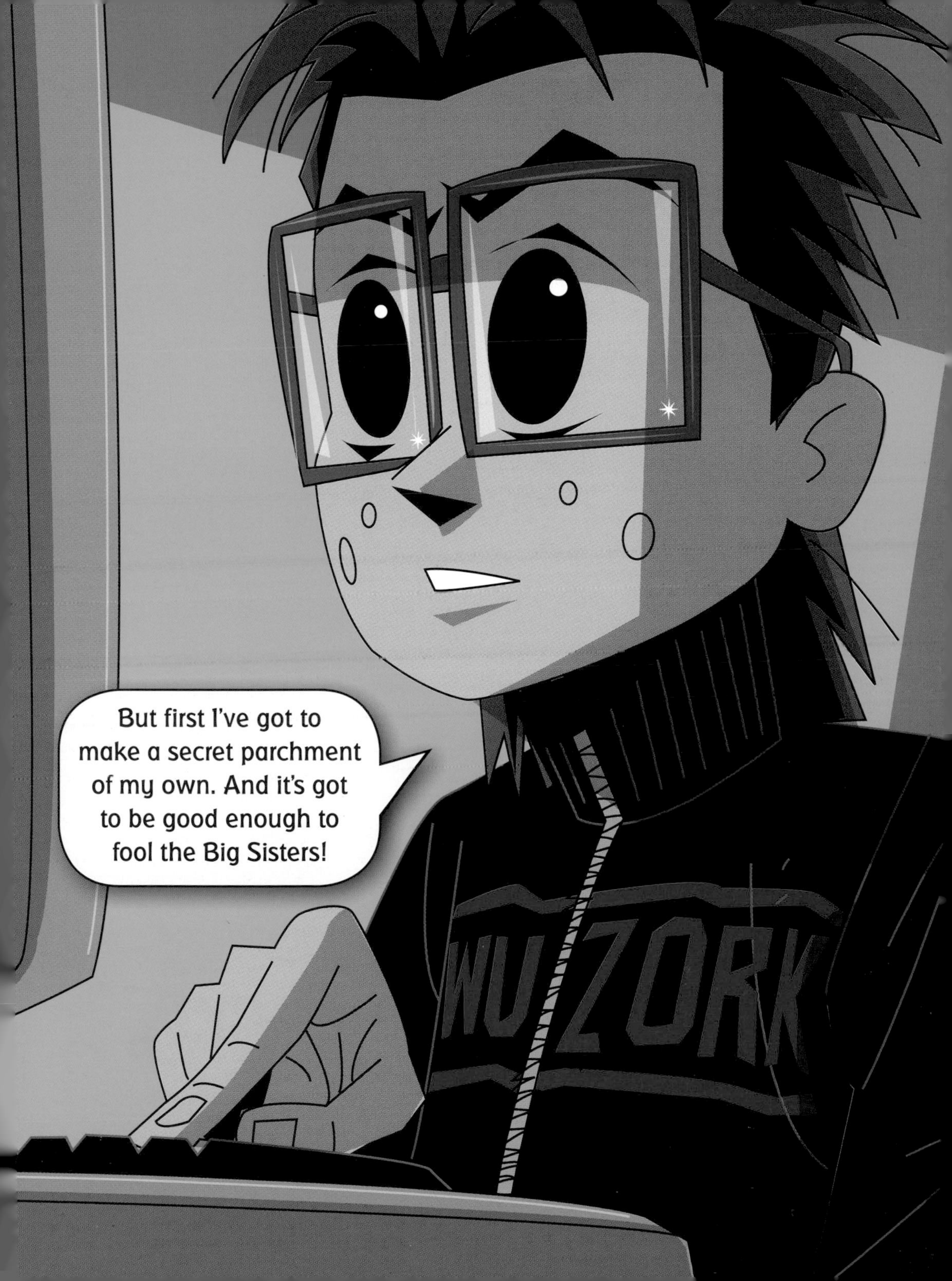
But first I've got to make a secret parchment of my own. And it's got to be good enough to fool the Big Sisters!
WU ZORK

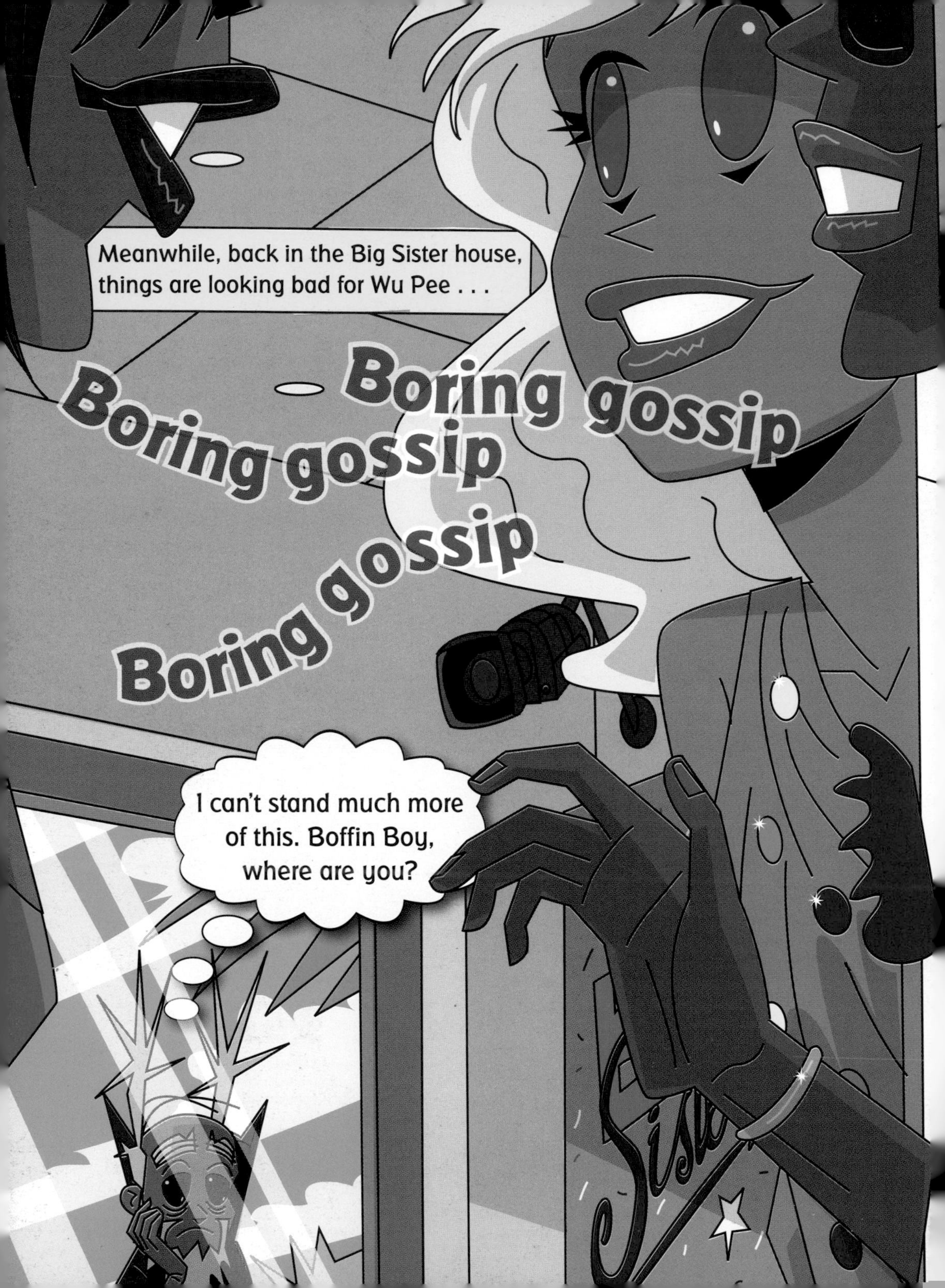

Meanwhile, back in the Big Sister house, things are looking bad for Wu Pee . . .
Boring gossip
Boring gossip
Boring gossip
Boring gossip
I can't stand much more of this. Boffin Boy, where are you?

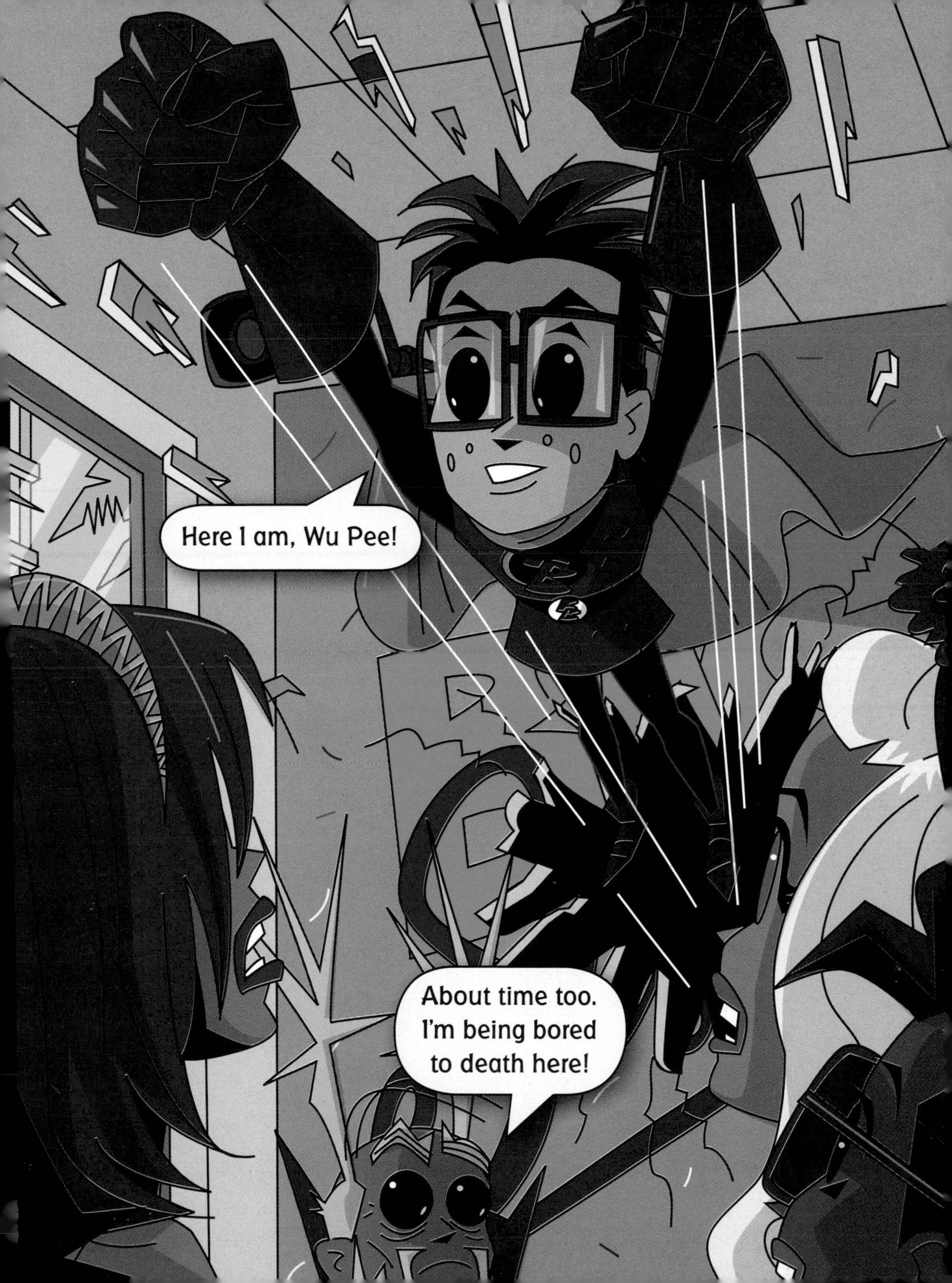
Here I am, Wu Pee!
About time too. I'm being bored to death here!

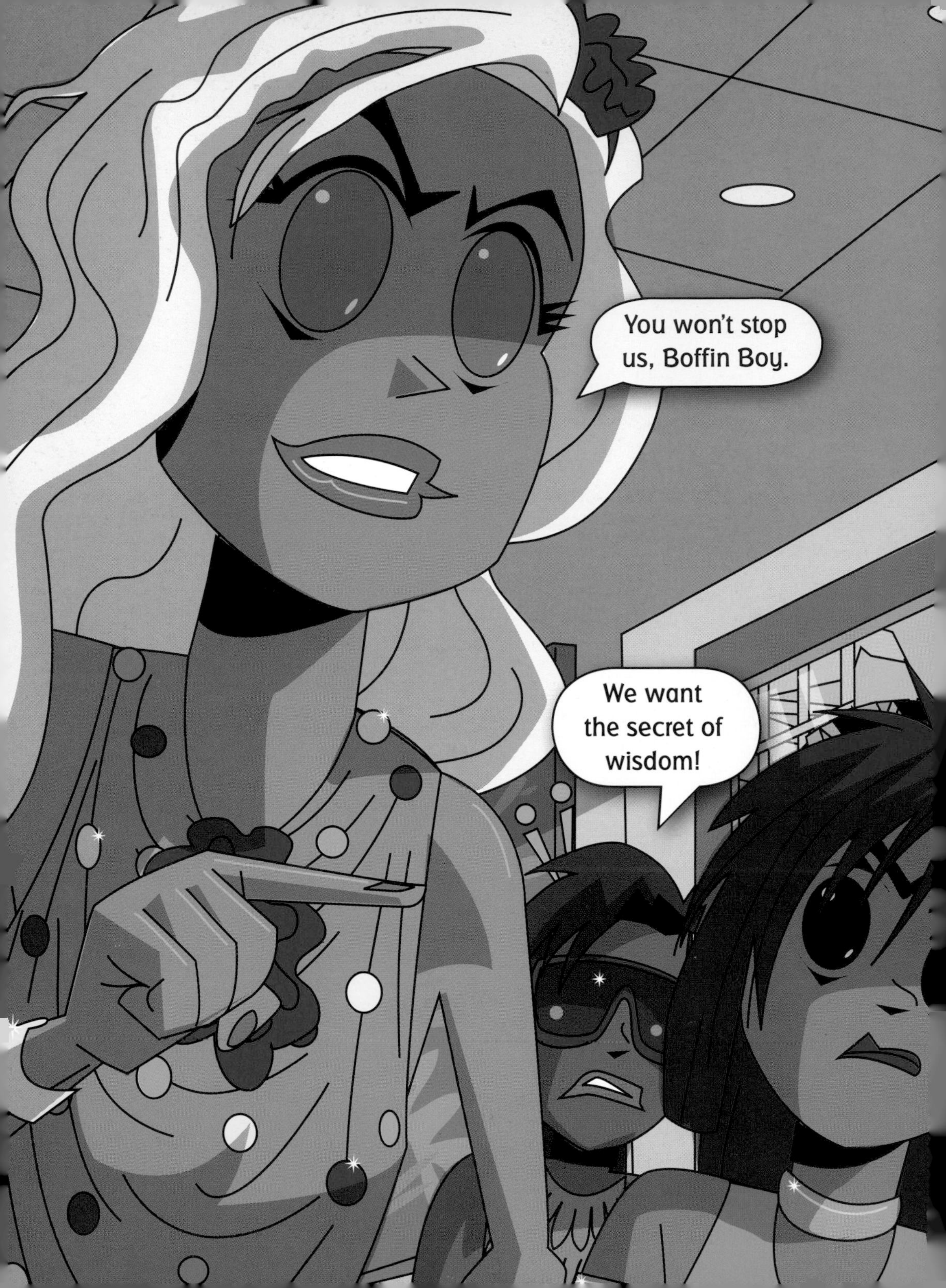
You won't stop us, Boffin Boy.
We want the secret of wisdom!

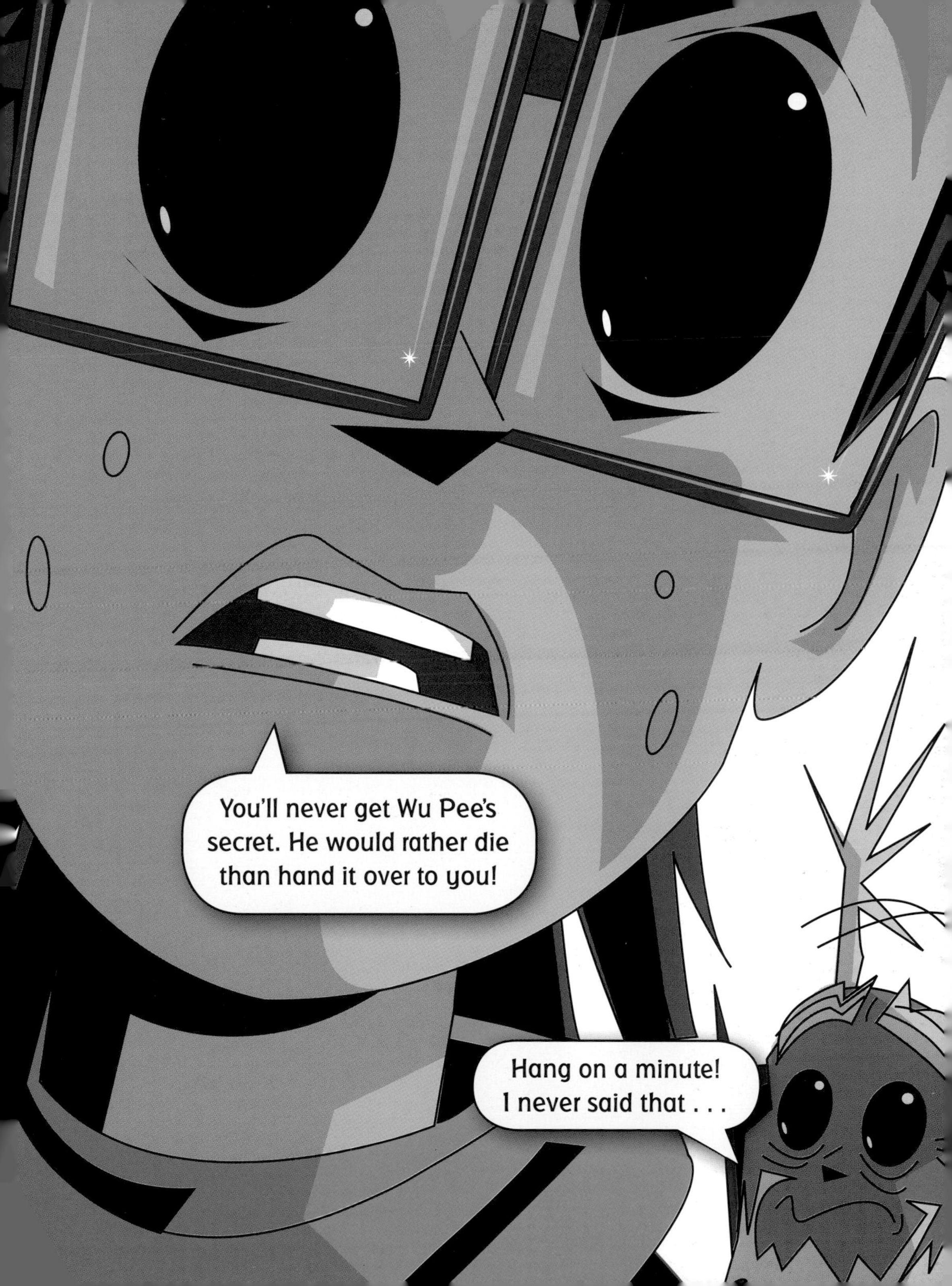
You'll never get Wu Pee's secret. He would rather die than hand it over to you!
Hang on a minute! I never said that . . .

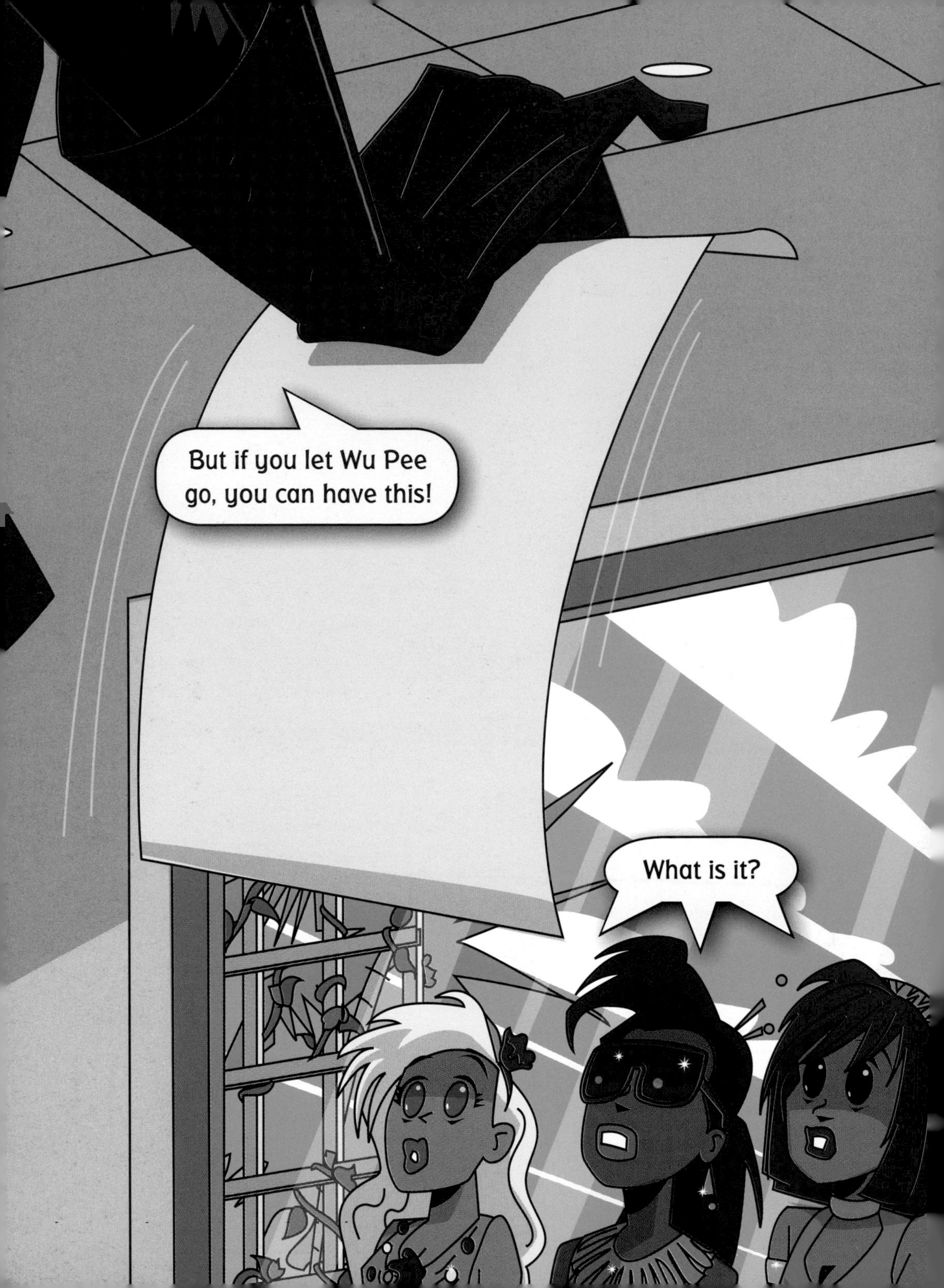
But if you let Wu Pee go, you can have this!
What is it?

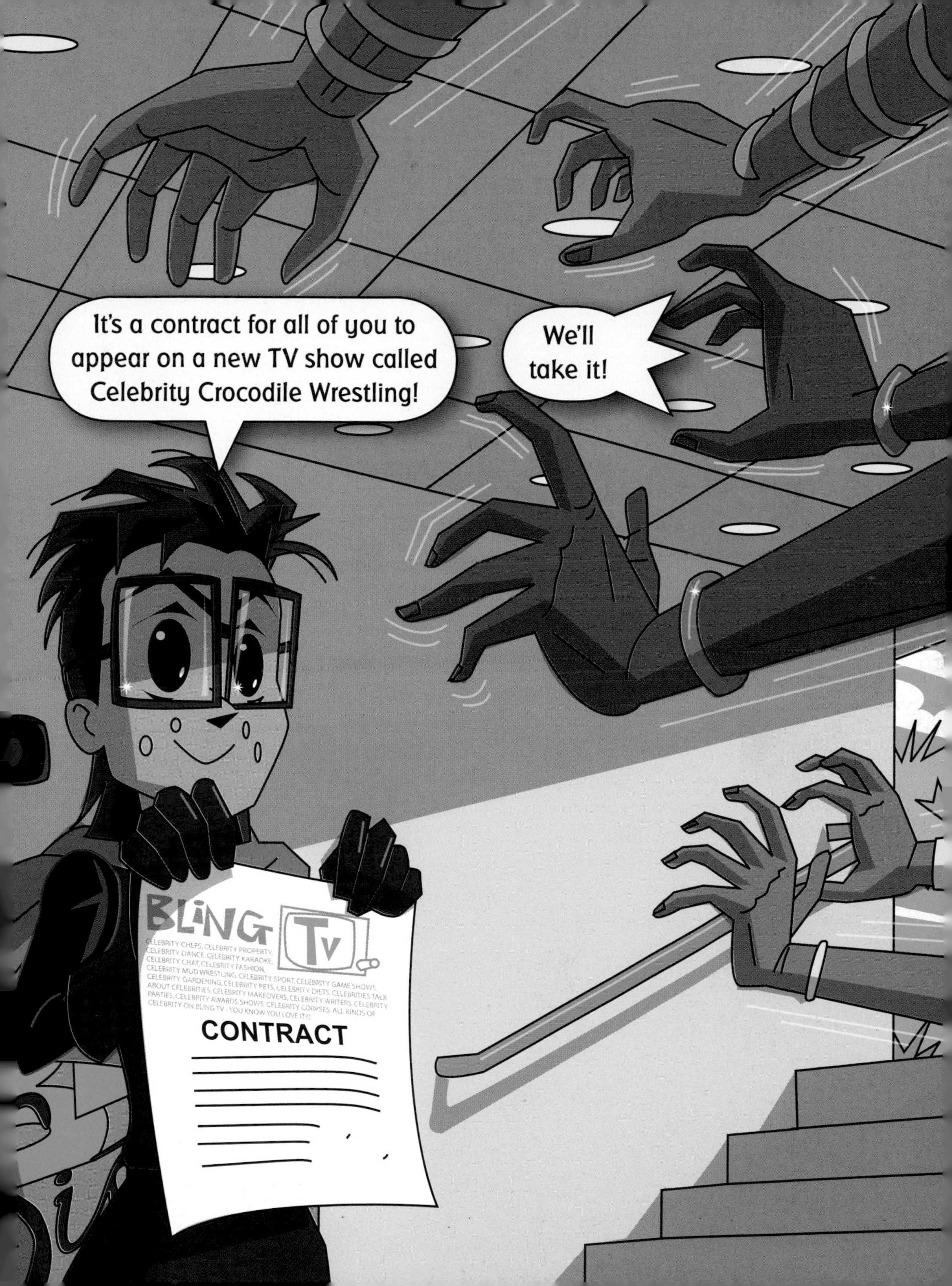
It's a contract for all of you to appear on a new TV show called Celebrity Crocodile Wrestling!
We'll take it!
BLING TV
CELEBRITY CHEFS, CELEBRITY PROPERTY, CELEBRITY DANCE, CELEBRITY KARAOKE, CELEBRITY CHAT, CELEBRITY FASHION, CELEBRITY MUD WRESTLING, CELEBRITY SPORT, CELEBRITY GAME SHOWS, CELEBRITY GARDENING, CELEBRITY PETS, CELEBRITY DIETS, CELEBRITIES TALK ABOUT CELEBRITIES, CELEBRITY MAKEOVERS, CELEBRITY WRITERS, CELEBRITY PARTIES, CELEBRITY AWARDS SHOWS, CELEBRITY CORPSES. ALL KINDS OF CELEBRITY ON BLING TV - YOU KNOW YOU LOVE IT!!
CONTRACT

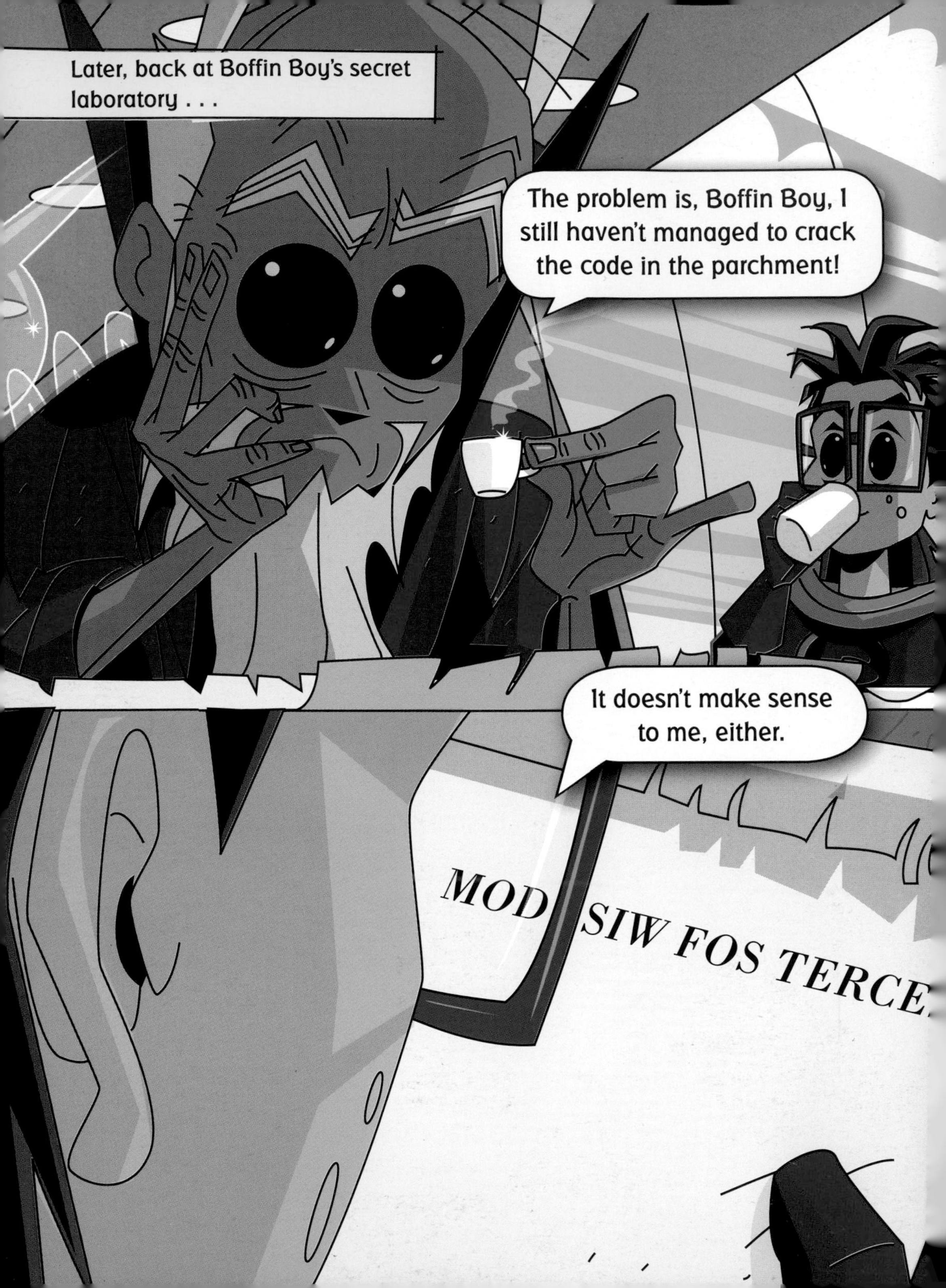
Later, back at Boffin Boy's secret laboratory . . .
The problem is, Boffin Boy, I still haven't managed to crack the code in the parchment!
It doesn't make sense to me, either.
MOD SIW FOS TERCE

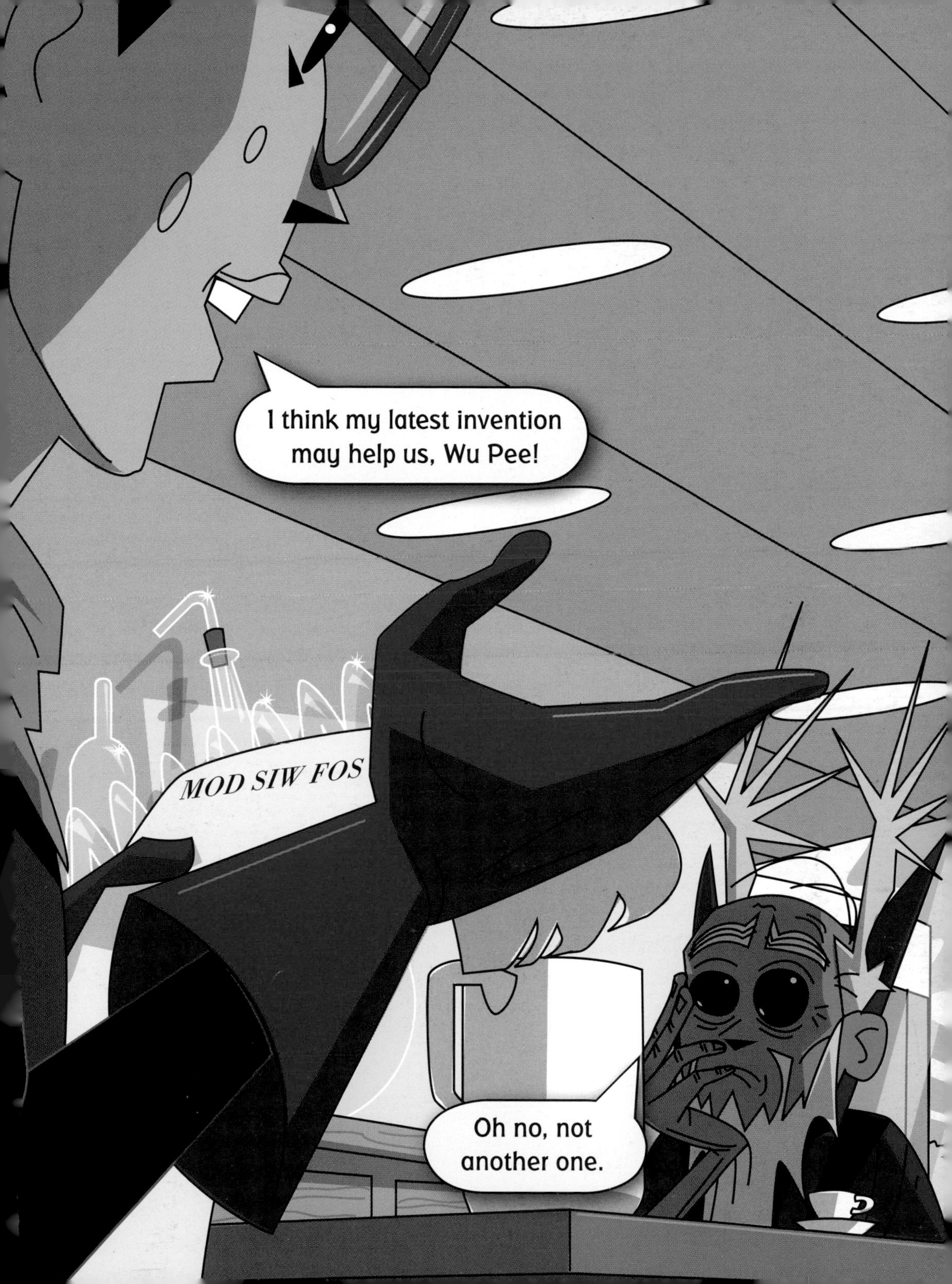
I think my latest invention may help us, Wu Pee!
MOD SIW FOS
Oh no, not another one.

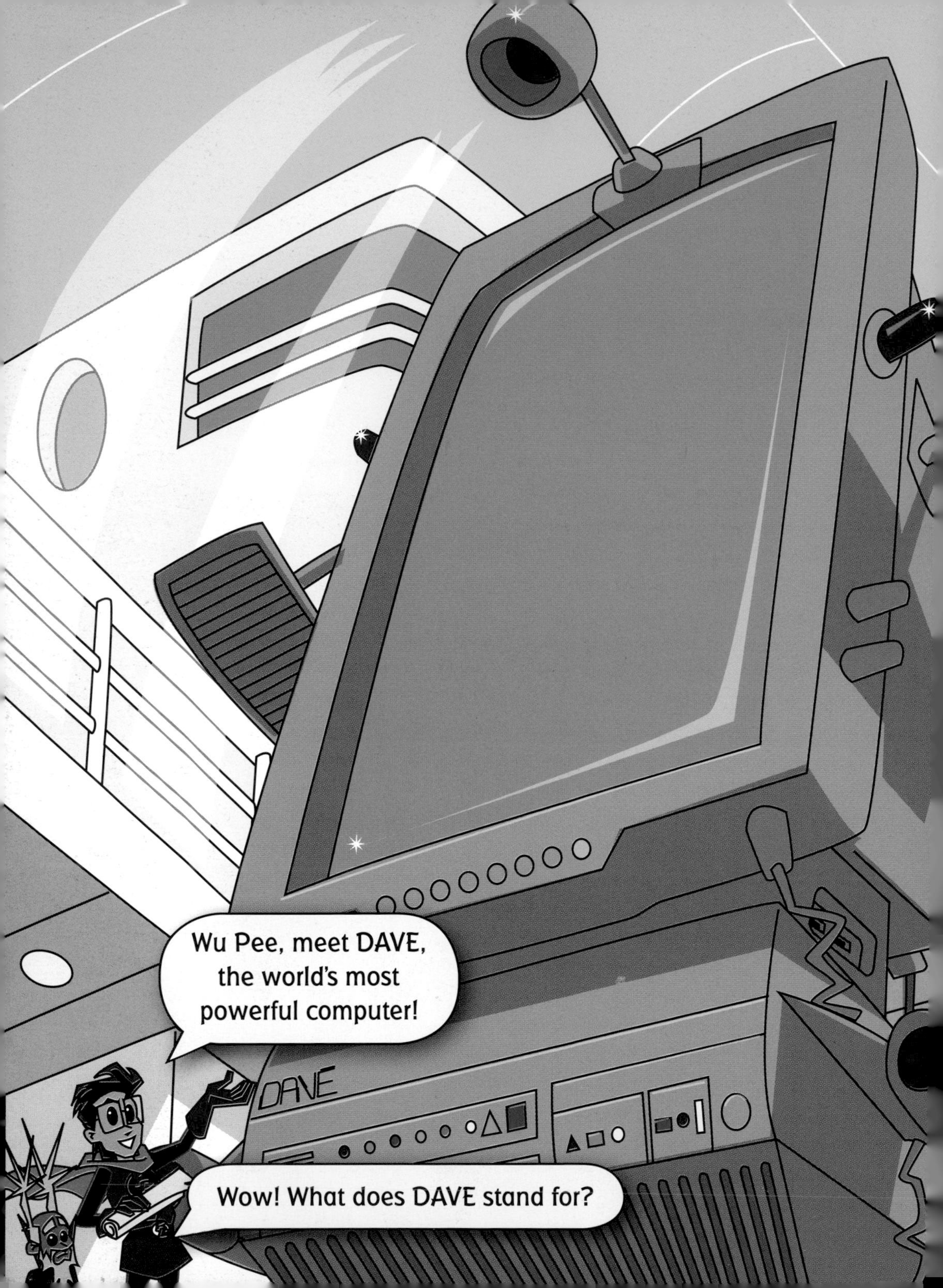
Wu Pee, meet DAVE, the world's most powerful computer!
DAVE
Wow! What does DAVE stand for?

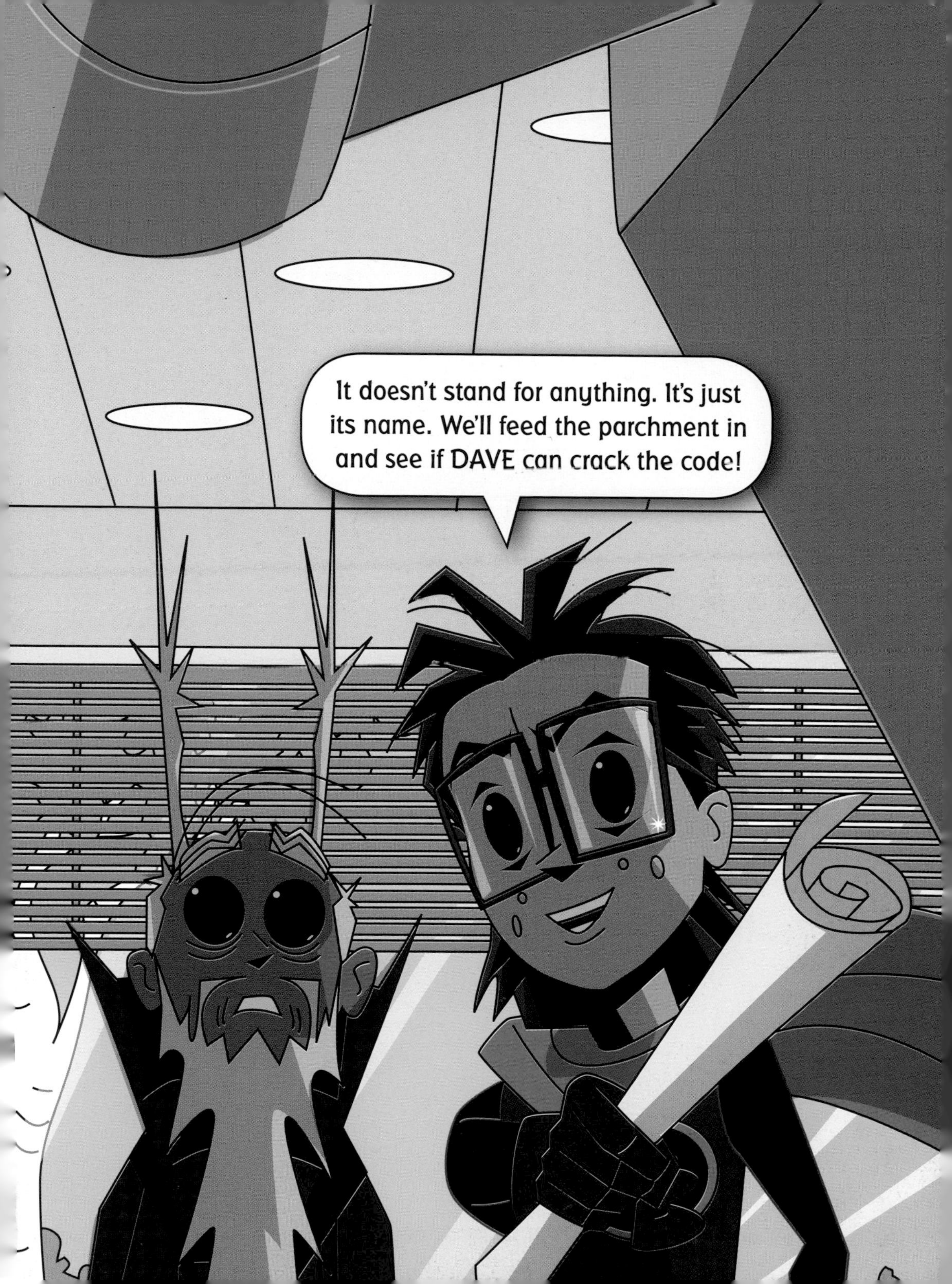
It doesn't stand for anything. It's just its name. We'll feed the parchment in and see if DAVE can crack the code!

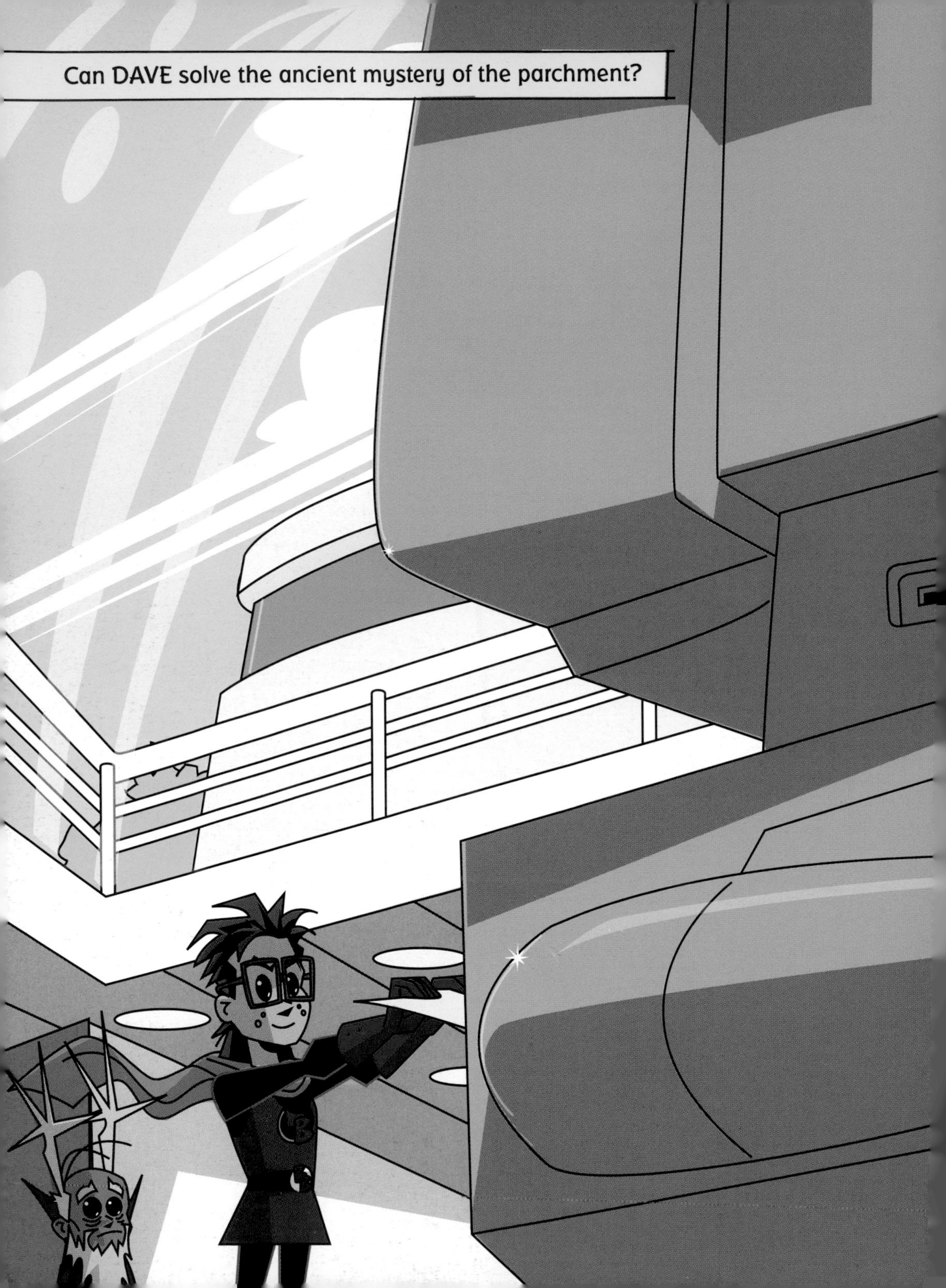
Can DAVE solve the ancient mystery of the parchment?

... SEARCH ME
DAVE

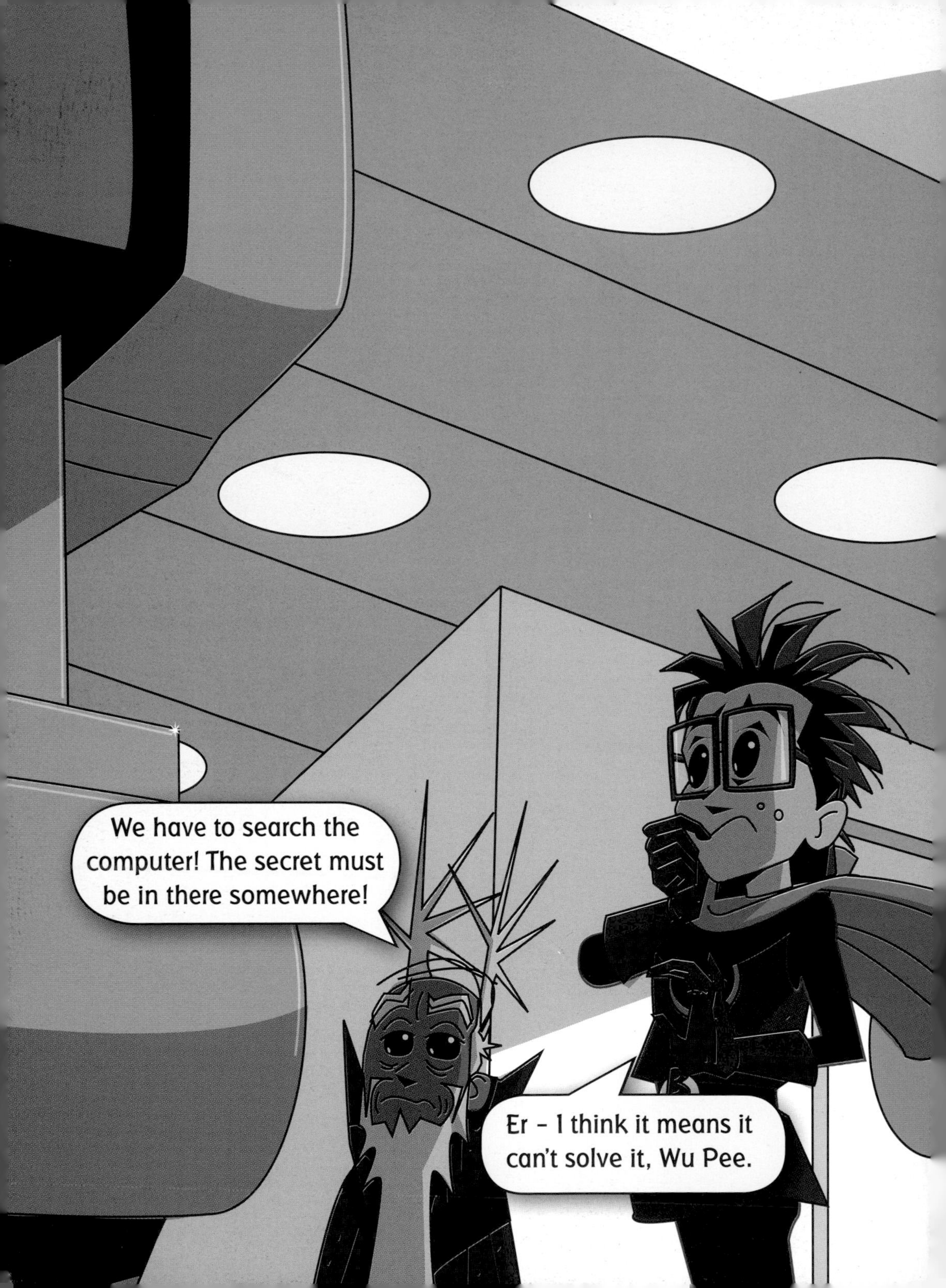
We have to search the computer! The secret must be in there somewhere!
Er – I think it means it can't solve it, Wu Pee.

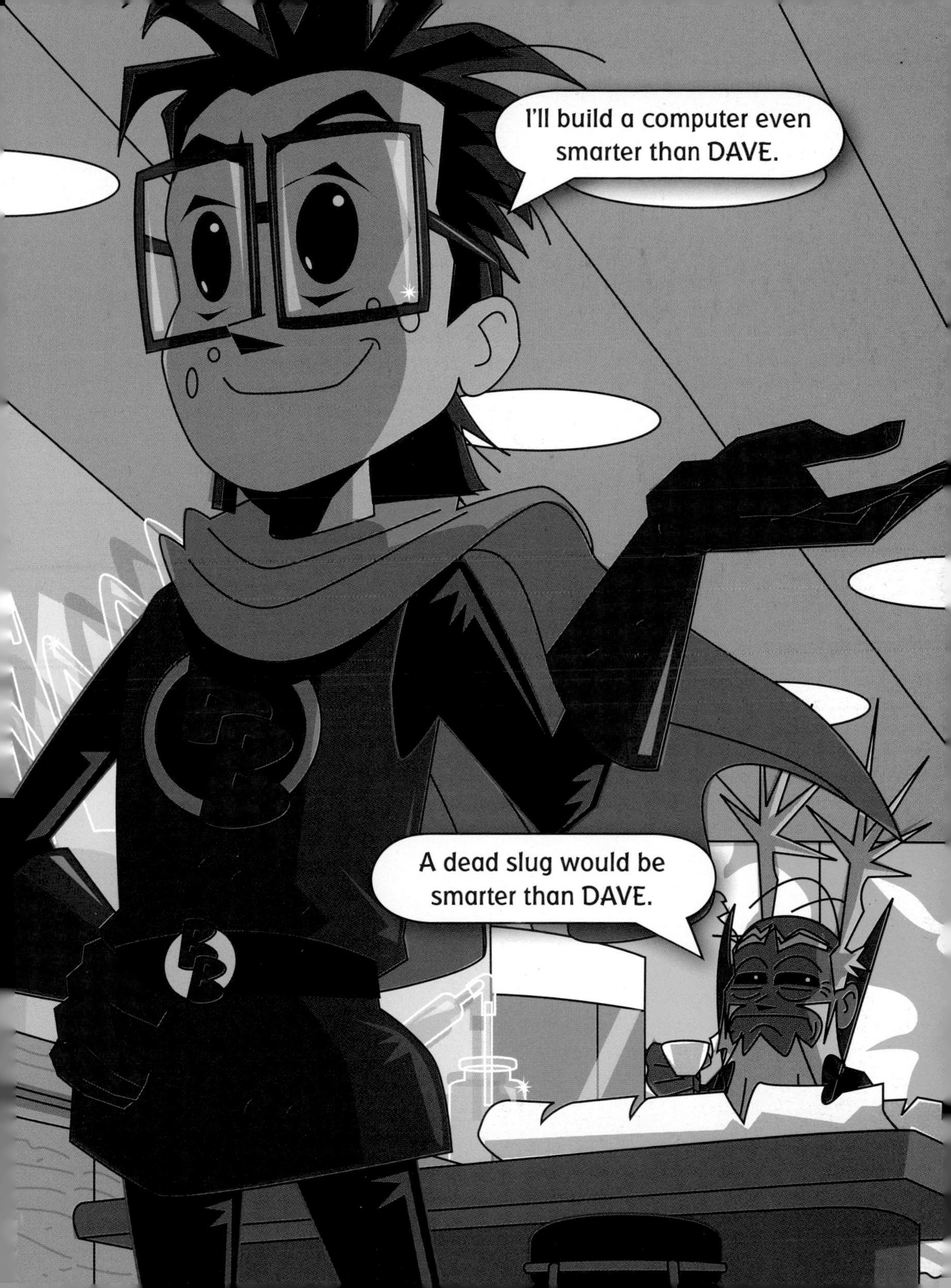
I'll build a computer even smarter than DAVE.
A dead slug would be smarter than DAVE.

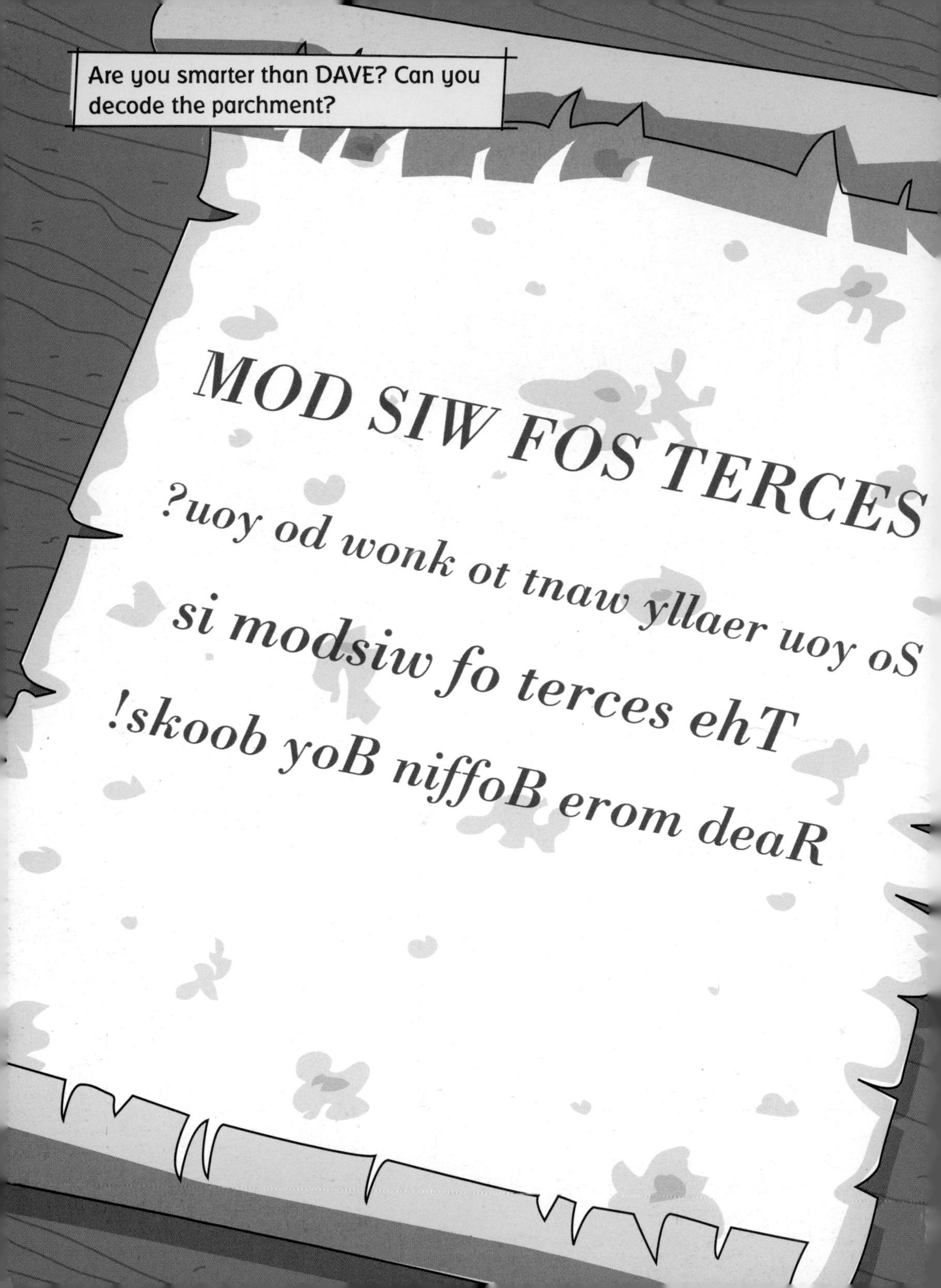
Are you smarter than DAVE? Can you decode the parchment?
MOD SIW FOS TERCES
?uoy od wonk ot tnaw yllaer uoy oS
si modsiw fo terces ehT
!skoob yoB niffoB erom deaR

ABOUT THE AUTHOR

David Orme has written over 200 books including poetry collections, fiction and non-fiction, and school text books. When he is not writing books he travels around the UK, giving performances, running writing workshops and courses.

Find out more at:
www.magic-nation.com.